ANIMAL
CRACKERS

A MEDAL FOR POPPY

ROSE IMPEY ★ SHOO RAYNER

ORCHARD BOOKS

ORCHARD BOOKS
338 Euston Road, London NW1 3BH
Orchard Books Australia
Hachette Children's Books
Level 17/207 Kent Street, Sydney NSW 2000

First published by Orchard Books in 1998
This edition published in 2009

Text © Rose Impey 1998
Illustrations © Shoo Rayner 2003

A CIP catalogue record for this book is available from the British Library.

ISBN 978 1 40830 510 2

1 3 5 7 9 10 8 6 4 2
Printed in China

Orchard Books is a division of Hachette Children's Books,
an Hachette UK company.
www.hachette.co.uk

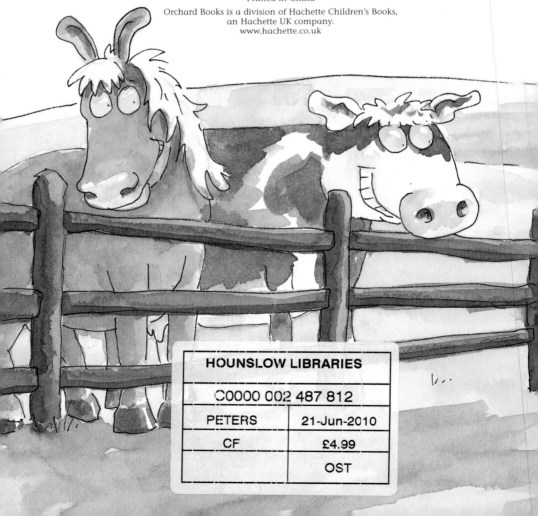

A Medal for Poppy

Old Man Brocksopp had a farm,
Eee-Aye, Eee-Aye, *Yow!*
And on that farm he had two dogs,
and a sheep and a horse and a cow.

And a hen and a goose and a goat,
and a son called Dan,
with a wife called Nan,
and their little girl, Lucy-Anne.

And he also had a remarkable pig
called Poppy.

Everyone on the farm liked Poppy.
She was clever and kind
and very brave.

Sheep wasn't brave.
Sheep was scared of lots of things:
the farm dogs barking at her heels,

bright lights,

bang!

loud noises.

Even Sheep's shadow made her shiver.

Oh, dear, oh, dear, my poor old nerves.

"Fancy being afraid of your own shadow," thought Poppy.

Horse was braver than Sheep.
But even Horse hid his head
in the hay when there was
thunder and lightning.

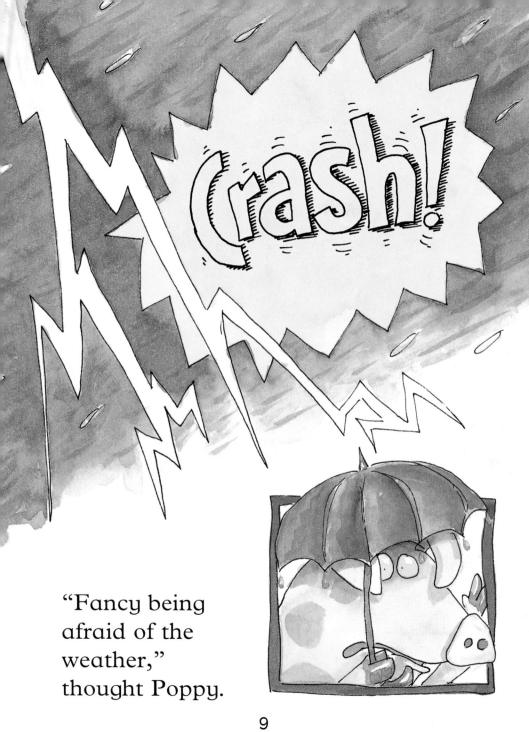

"Fancy being
afraid of the
weather,"
thought Poppy.

Cow wasn't afraid of loud noises
or bright lights.
But Cow *was* afraid of the dark.
She didn't make a fuss about it.
She just moved up closer to her
friends when darkness came.

"Fancy being afraid
of the dark,"
thought Poppy.

Poppy wasn't afraid of
bright lights
or loud noises
or being alone in the dark.
Poppy was a plucky pig.
Everybody said so.

They said so when Poppy chased the fox away when he tried to gobble up Goose's goslings!

They said so when she rescued Cow from cattle rustlers.

They said so when she saved Hen's eggs, the day the barn caught fire.

Poppy liked to do brave deeds.
She liked being told what a
plucky pig she was.

But there *was* one thing Poppy
was afraid of:
Old Man Brocksopp's pond.

Once, when Poppy was a piglet,
she'd tried to walk on water.
And she'd never forgotten it.
So Poppy kept well away from
the farm pond.

Each day, when the sun was hot, the other animals gathered round the pond to feel the cool breeze coming off the water.
But Poppy didn't join them.

If Poppy had to go on errands across
the farm, she took the longest route,
rather than pass by the pond.

No one seemed to notice.
No one guessed Poppy's secret.
Why would they?
After all, pigs don't swim, do they?

One day, Poppy had a nasty surprise.
Old Man Brocksopp was sitting in
the yard, reading his paper.

In the paper there was a picture
of a pig, just like her.
But this pig was swimming!
"What do you think of that?"
said the farmer.
Poppy didn't know what to
think of it.
But it made her blood run cold.

That night Poppy dreamed about
the swimming pig.
She woke up in a cold sweat.
And every night that week
she had the same dream.

Poppy didn't feel at all happy.
Everyone else still thought
she was a plucky pig.
But Poppy didn't feel plucky;
she *felt* scared.

She wanted to tell someone,
but she couldn't.
Then she thought of Goat.

Goat was old and wise.
Goat would help.
Poppy decided to talk to her.
Goat didn't seem at all surprised.
"Oh, my dear," she said.
"Everyone's scared of something."
"Are they?" said Poppy.

Of course. The brave animals are the ones who are scared - but don't show it. Like cow.

"Cow?" said Poppy.
"Yes," said Goat. "Cow hates the dark and she has to face it every night. That's what I call brave: knowing what you're afraid of, but *not* letting it get the better of you."

Poppy went away and thought
about Goat's words.
She knew what she had to do.
The next day Poppy went to join
her friends by the pond.
Each day she moved closer
and closer to the water,
until she didn't feel so afraid.

Monday

Tuesday

Wednesday

Thursday

Friday

It was quite a hard thing to do,
but Poppy didn't tell anyone.
It was her secret.

Slowly she began to feel brave again.
She began to feel like a plucky pig.
Then, one day, something terrible
happened.

All the animals were beside
the pond, as usual.

Old Man Brocksopp was in the
far field cutting the hay.

Dan was in the shed mending
the tractor.

Nan was in the farmhouse
paying the bills.

No one was watching little
Lucy-Anne.
No one noticed her
toddling
across
the yard
heading
straight for
the pond.

Poppy and all her friends were
snoozing in the midday sun.
Even the ducks were dreaming.
No one noticed little Lucy-Anne
trying to toddle on water.

But suddenly they heard her.
Suddenly everyone was wide awake.
Suddenly everyone went wild.

All the animals started up,
bleating and clucking
and mooing and neighing.
They didn't know what else to do,
so they all *panicked*.

But Poppy didn't panic.
She knew that someone
had to save the little girl.
Poppy, the plucky little pig,
who was *still afraid of water*,
jumped right in and
started to swim.

Poppy didn't know how she did it.
She just did it.
She kicked her little legs
and swam to the rescue.

Poppy opened her mouth
and fixed her teeth on
little Lucy-Anne's clothes
and towed her to the side.

The other animals had made
so much noise that everyone
had come running.
Nan was there,

and Dan was there.

Even Old Man Brocksopp
had heard them in the far field.
Everyone was there to see Poppy,
the pluckiest pig in the world,
save little Lucy-Anne from drowning.

Give that pig a medal.

None of them realised why this
was Poppy's bravest deed of all,
except Goat, of course.
And Goat knew how to keep a secret.

Crack-A-Joke

What do pigs use to
write to their friends?
Pen and oink!

What do you give a sick pig?
Oinkment!

What do you call a
story about pigs?
A pig tail!

Waiter, this stew
isn't fit for a pig!

Would sir like me
to take it away
and fetch him
some that is?

What happens when pigs fly?
The price of bacon goes up!

Why is getting up at
three o'clock in the
morning like a pig's tail?
It's twirly.

What do you call a
thief that breaks into
a hamburger factory?
A hamburglar!

ANIMAL
CRACKERS

COLLECT ALL THE
ANIMAL CRACKERS BOOKS!

A Birthday for Bluebell	978 1 40830 293 4	£4.99
Too Many Babies	978 1 40830 294 1	£4.99
Hot Dog Harris	978 1 40830 295 8	£4.99
Sleepy Sammy	978 1 40830 296 5	£4.99
Precious Potter	978 1 40830 297 2	£4.99
Phew Sidney	978 1 40830 298 9	£4.99
Open Wide Wilbur	978 1 40830 299 6	£4.99
We Want William	978 1 40830 300 9	£4.99
Welcome Home, Barney!	978 1 40830 513 3	£4.99
A Medal For Poppy	978 1 40830 510 2	£4.99
A Fortune For Yo-Yo	978 1 40830 509 6	£4.99
Long Live Roberto	978 1 40830 512 6	£4.99
Rhode Island Roy	978 1 40830 514 0	£4.99
Tiny Tim	978 1 40830 508 9	£4.99
Pipe Down, Prudle!	978 1 40830 511 9	£4.99
Stella's Staying Put	978 1 40830 515 7	£4.99

All priced at £4.99

Orchard Colour Crunchies are available from all good bookshops, or can be
ordered direct from the publisher:
Orchard Books, PO BOX 29, Douglas IM99 1BQ
Credit card orders please telephone 01624 836000
or fax 01624 837033 or visit our internet site: www.orchardbooks.co.uk
or e-mail: bookshop@enterprise.net for details.
To order please quote title, author and ISBN
and your full name and address.
Cheques and postal orders should be made payable to 'Bookpost plc.'
Postage and packing is FREE within the UK
(overseas customers should add £2.00 per book).
Prices and availability are subject to change.